JUST BECAUSE
ADOPTED . . .

A story about adoption and forever love

P. Shiroma, Psy. D.

illustrations by Isabel Nadal

Printed in the United States of America

First Printing, April 2021

ISBN 9798591581473

Library of Congress Control Number: 2021906869

TONBO
PRESS

www.DrPShiroma.com

This book belongs to

_____

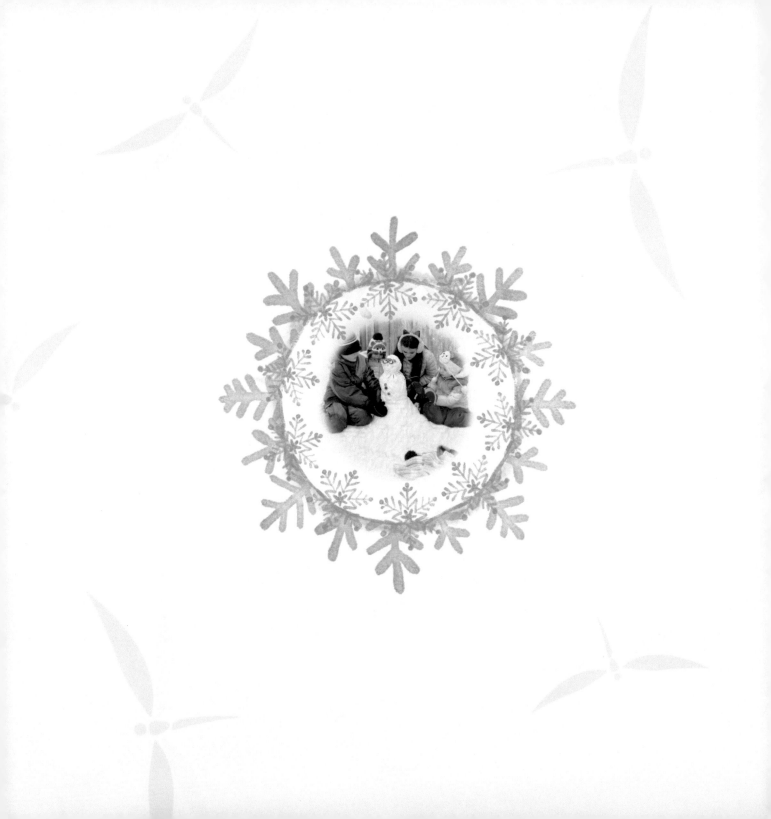

For my husband, who rode along the adoption journey through the highs and lows to complete our forever family. For being a devoted Daddy to our beautiful children and for making anything possible. With all my love, P.

"It's snowing! I'm going outside to play with Yuki!" shouted William, running to the front door.

"Don't forget your warm coat, mittens, and snow boots!" reminded his mother from the kitchen.

"I already have my coat, mittens, and boots on, Mom," muttered William, and he hurried out through the bright red front door.

Today was the first snowfall of the year, and he didn't want to miss a second of it!

Yuki ran towards William and shouted, "I love playing in the snow!"
William smiled and nodded as they gave each other high fives.
Since they had become best friends, this had been their
signature greeting.

William looked at the white snow all around them. He asked excitedly, "What should we do first?"

"Let's have a snowball fight!" suggested Yuki, forming a snowball behind his back.

"Awesome!" Before William could finish talking, Yuki had surprised him with a snowball to the chest.

The boys chased each other around, throwing snowballs and laughing until they fell into the snow, out of breath.

"Let's do snow angels next," Yuki anticipated, moving his arms and legs.

William hinted, "I have a better idea! Let's make snow families!"

"I like that idea," Yuki chuckled.

"I'll grab some colorful scarves from home," William said.

Without hesitation, Yuki added, "I can get different hats for us too."

"Let's meet back here in five minutes," William quickly responded.

William and Yuki ran into their homes and returned minutes later with their arms full of scarves and hats.

They rubbed their warm snow mitten-covered hands anxiously and started building their snow families.

While the boys were creating their masterpieces, Rosie, the new girl next door, quietly approached William.

"Hi, William!" Rosie loudly screeched in her high-pitched voice.

William was startled and fell face-first onto the snowball he had been molding.

Yuki and Rosie laughed while William spluttered and stood back up, saying in a trembling voice, "Hey Rosie."

Rosie looked at what her friends were creating and asked curiously, "What are you doing?"

"We're making our snow families. Want to play with us?" invited William.

Rosie smiled. "Sure, sounds fun!"

"I'm making my father first since he's the tallest in our family," Yuki explained, picking up a hat from the snow. "This tall blue hat is perfect for him!"

Rosie tapped a finger on her cheek thoughtfully. Then, with a big smile, she declared, "I'm an only child. I'll make myself first!"

Rosie began to gather snow and spotted something pretty on the snow-covered ground.

Her eyes twinkled as she picked it up and said, "This pink scarf will be perfect. Pink is my favorite color!"

William grinned from ear to ear, then said, "I'm making my sisters and then my Mom and Dad. I'll make myself last."

"Why are you making your sisters?" Yuki asked, surprised. "They're not your real sisters."

"Why are they not my real sisters?" William asked, confused.

Rosie stopped sculpting the snow and glanced at her new friends with wide eyes.

Yuki expressed, "You're adopted, so that's not your real family."

"Just because I was adopted doesn't mean my family isn't my real family," William said, feeling heartbroken by Yuki's hurtful words.

Yuki and Rosie were having fun, making their snow families, and commenting on each other's creations.

But William sat in front of his half-finished snow family, lost in thought.

Then he whispered, "I'll only make myself."

"Making snow families isn't fun, after all," William thought.

He destroyed the half-finished figures of his snow sisters and started up again, but this time he is far less excited.

William's Dad was shoveling the soft snow along the long narrow driveway when he noticed that William seemed unhappy.

He put down his snow shovel and walked toward William and his friends. "What are you all making?" William's Dad asked, pretending not to notice William's sad face.

"We're making our snow families," answered Rosie.
"That's so creative!" William's Dad replied.

"Who are you working on now, Yuki?" William's Dad asked.

"I'm building my mother! I have finished making my father already," Yuki boasted while tying a bright yellow polka-dotted scarf around his snow-mother's neck.

Turning to Rosie, William's Dad grinned, "That looks just like you. The cutest snow-Rosie!"

Rosie giggled and did a little twirl, "Thank you!"

All the while, William was shuffling his feet and looking down at the snow.

"What about you, William? Who are you building?" William's Dad asked.

"I was making my sisters," William said, not looking up.

"But William doesn't have a real family because he was adopted, so he just decided to make himself," Yuki blurted out when William said nothing else.

"I see," William's Dad replied, scratching his head.

"You're right! William was adopted. But he does have a family that includes his parents and three sisters," William's Dad explained.

"What does 'adopted' mean?" Rosie eagerly asked.

"Adopted means that William was born to other parents. We call them his birth parents," William's Dad calmly explained. "They loved him very much but wanted to allow William to have everything that they couldn't provide for him at that time in their lives.

His birth parents wanted to find the perfect and most supportive family to care for William and love him unconditionally, just as they loved him.

Adoption was a difficult decision to make, but they had William's best interests at heart. The reason his birth parents carefully chose us to adopt him."

As William's Dad talked, the children sat in the snow and listened attentively.

He continued, "Our family wouldn't be complete without William or his sisters.

We love them because families are forever, regardless of being born or adopted into one. Isn't that what families are all about?"

William proudly held his head high with the happiest expression on his face and gave his Dad the best fist bump ever.

Yuki said, "I understand adoption better now."

"I do, too," added Rosie. She leaned towards William's Dad, "Thank you for explaining to us what adoption means."

Embarrassed, Yuki said, "I'm sorry for saying you didn't have a real family, William."

"That's okay! You're still my best friend," William said, giving Yuki a high five.

"Now that Yuki and I know more about adoption, can we finish making our snow family?" Rosie asked impatiently.

William happily gave his friends two thumbs up.

William's Dad waved goodbye. He realized his son was happy as he walked back to his driveway to continue shoveling the snow, "I look forward to seeing your finished work of art!" he said with anticipation.

The children worked for the rest of the afternoon on their masterpieces while laughing and exchanging funny jokes.

Finally, they completed all three snow families.

William's Dad announced, "Those are the best Forever Snow Families ever made! Good job!"

William, Yuki, and Rosie beamed, pleased by his compliment.

"What should we play next?" Yuki asked.

"Let's have another snowball fight!" William said playfully, picking up some snow when tiny new snowflakes began falling.

Thank you for purchasing this book. I sincerely hope you enjoyed the story as much as I enjoyed writing it. I would truly appreciate a short review on the site you purchased this book or your favorite book website. Reviews are crucial for any author, and even just a line or two can make a huge difference. Your opinion matters and is very much appreciated. Thank you.

www.DrPShiroma.com